The Story of Passover

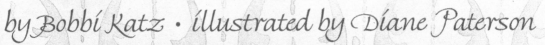

by Bobbi Katz · illustrated by Diane Paterson

A Random House PICTUREBACK® Shape Book

Published in the United States by Random House, Inc., New York, and simultaneously
in Canada by Random House of Canada Limited, Toronto.
Library of Congress Catalog Card Number: 95-68224   ISBN: 0-679-87038-5

Manufactured in the United States of America   10 9 8 7 6 5 4 3 2 1

Random House 🏠 New York

*W*hen the snow melts and robins start to chirp, spring is on the way. It's time to put away ice skates and sleds and take out kites and bicycles.

And for Jewish families, it's time to start preparing for the holiday of Passover. In this weeklong celebration, Jews remember both the bitterness of slavery and the sweetness of freedom.

Passover begins on the fifteenth night of the Jewish month of Nisan, which comes in late March or early April.

In the days before Passover, many Jewish families give their homes a spring cleaning. They also pack away all their dishes, silverware, and pots and pans. During Passover, Jewish families eat special foods prepared with just-for-Passover utensils and served on just-for-Passover dishes.

Passover starts with a festive meal called a *Seder,* which means "order" in Hebrew. The story of Passover is read aloud from a book called the *Haggadah*. The Haggadah is a guide to the Seder, and it also contains songs and prayers.

The family gathers at the table to relive the story of the first Passover by eating, drinking, and reciting prayers, according to the Haggadah.

Over 3,000 years ago, the Jews were living in Egypt. They were welcome there and life was good. They worshiped the Lord in freedom. Then a *pharaoh,* or king, came to power who decided to make the Jews his slaves. Jews were forced to work from dawn to sunset making bricks and building huge palaces and grand cities for the Pharaoh.

One day the Pharaoh decided that all Jewish boy babies must be killed. The parents tried to hide their boy babies, wherever and however they could.

Pharaoh's daughter found one Jewish baby hidden in a tiny cradle among the tall rushes that grew near the river Nile. She called the baby Moses and found a Jewish woman to care for him.

When Moses grew up, the Lord said that He would help him lead the Jewish people to freedom. The Lord gave Moses signs to prove His power: a bush burst into flames and a stick turned into a snake.

Although Moses was shy, he became a brave messenger for the Lord.
He went to the Pharaoh and said, "Let my people go!"
Pharaoh just laughed. He had armies! The Jews were powerless slaves.
Pharaoh ordered the taskmasters to make the Jews work even harder.

But the Lord was more powerful than the Pharaoh. One by one He sent plagues to Egypt to make the Pharaoh change his mind.

The first plague turned all the water in the ponds and rivers to blood.

Then thick clouds of flies buzzed everywhere.

Frogs leapt out of the ponds and into the Egyptians' ovens and beds.

After that came a plague of itchy, ouchy boils.

Next thunder boomed and hail pounded the earth, crushing the plants.

And then locusts arrived to eat everything the hail hadn't destroyed.
The Lord made the Egyptians' days as dark as a moonless night.
With each plague, the Pharaoh told Moses that the Jews could leave.
But as soon as the plague stopped, Pharaoh would change his mind.

Finally, the Lord told Moses that He would send the Angel of Death to kill the firstborn child of all the Egyptian families. The Lord told Moses to have the Jewish families mark the doorposts of their houses with the blood of the lamb they sacrificed to Him each spring. That would be a sign to the Angel of Death to *pass over* their homes, which is how the holiday of Passover got its name.

When this last plague started, Pharaoh said to Moses, "Take your people and leave now!" And that's just what Moses did.

The Jews grabbed the bread they were preparing before it even had a chance to rise and hurried into the wilderness. The Lord guided them with a cloud by day and a pillar of fire by night.

Just as they reached the Red Sea, they saw that Pharaoh's army was not far behind. Pharaoh had changed his mind again! But then a miracle happened! The Lord made a dry path in between the swirling waves of the sea, and Moses led the Jews safely across. But when the Egyptians tried to follow them, the waters closed. The Jews were free at last!

And ever since that time, Jewish families thank the Lord for the miracle of their own freedom and pray for the freedom of others.

A special Seder plate contains symbols of the first Passover. Bitter herbs, like horseradish, remind Jews of the bitterness of slavery. Parsley dipped in salt water recalls the tears their ancestors shed. A roasted shankbone reminds them of the lamb that was sacrificed. *Charoset*, a mixture of chopped apples, nuts, and a little wine, looks like the mortar once spread between the bricks of Pharaoh's cities. And an egg stands for spring—and new life.

According to the Haggadah, the youngest child at the Seder asks, "Why is this night different from all other nights?"

The answer is: On other nights we eat leavened or unleavened bread. Tonight we eat only *matzoh*.

And matzoh—flat, unleavened bread—is the most special Passover food. Three pieces of matzoh are placed on the table. Half of one piece, called the *afikomen*, is hidden somewhere in the house. At the end of the Seder, all the children try to find it. The lucky child who does gets a prize.

Matzoh is like the unleavened bread the Jews took with them when they followed Moses out of Egypt.

Jewish people eat no other bread but matzoh during the whole week of Passover, in order to remember just how precious freedom is.